# HOLIDAY RIDE

**EMMA BRAY**

# CHAPTER
# ONE

Emily

"UNBELIEVABLE," I mutter to myself.

I should have known there was an ulterior motive when my mom suggested this mother-daughter vacation. She claimed she was worried about me working so much and wanted me to take some time off with her. That alone should've tipped me off because my mother has always been too wrapped up in her latest flavor of the month to spend time with her daughter.

Disappointment stabs at me. I hoped this time would be different.

As What's-His-Name comes striding over to Mom with a big shit-eating grin on his face, I realize I've been duped once again. This was all orchestrated so my mom and her latest boy-toy could have a getaway on her daughter's dime.

My mom doesn't have much time to work between flirting with every man in sight. She was only profitable when she had a sugar daddy, but he caught her messing around with the pool boy, so there went that.

Does it sound like I'm calling my mother a slut? Because yeah, she is. I'm not shaming her or judging her. I'm just stating facts.

I watch as Mom and her boyfriend put on a small production of pretending they happened to run into each other and isn't this such a weird coincidence? They won't be winning any Oscars for their performances, but I'll give them an A for effort.

And here comes the good part. The dude mentions he doesn't have a room booked yet and looks sad when he adds, "They were all booked up."

Mom turns puppy dog eyes to me as she speaks to her boyfriend. "Well, you can stay with us! Right, honey?"

I paste a falsely bright smile on my face and reply as expected. "Of course!"

I booked a two-bedroom, but I'm not looking forward to the sounds of this dude fucking my mom non-stop because I know that's what's in the cards.

Mom is flushed, and he's getting handsy, grabbing her hips to pull her closer to him.

I purse my lips in irritation and head toward the cabin. I hear Mom and her boy-toy trailing along behind me.

I booked two weeks off to essentially be my mother's madam and set her up in a room where she can fuck the shit out of this guy.

He's murmuring to her, something I can't hear, and then she giggles—*giggles*—like a high school girl.

I have to fight to keep from rolling my eyes. What grown woman giggles? My forty-year-old mother, that's who.

When we reach the cabin, my mood sours further when I see the cabin has a queen bed and a room with two twin beds. It's technically two bedrooms, but it's meant for a family with kids.

My mother and her boy-toy take the master suite with the queen bed, so I'm stuck sleeping on a twin bed in the kids' suite. Not that I give a shit where I sleep, but it's the principle. I'm footing the bill for this trip, yet they plop their asses in the master suite without asking me if it's okay.

I wheel my suitcase into the room and fall onto the bed with a scowl when more of my mother's ridiculous giggling floats through the walls from the master suite. But it gets worse when the lusty moaning starts.

I grab a pillow and press it over my ears, but it does no good. I can still hear them. With a growl of frustration, I flounce up from the bed and retreat to the wrap-around porch.

When my mother lets out a piercing scream that leaves absolutely no doubt that lover boy has hit a home run, I can't take it anymore. I march off the porch to take a brief tour of the grounds.

Maybe they'll have worked it out of their systems by the time I get back.

Mother-daughter vacation, my ass.

———

Cole

"Sure thing, partner. Just call me whenever you're ready to book something," I say, handing over my flimsy business card to the guy in front of me.

"Cool. Thanks, man." The guy takes the card from me and stuffs it in the front pocket of his tropical tourist shirt before wrapping an arm around his woman and meandering off.

As much as I hate to admit it, my sister's idea of passing out these business cards has been a boon. We have more business than ever—especially when I come to Mountain Ridge Resort and pass the little fuckers out. It's a hell of a lot easier than repeatedly chanting my number to people.

I take a couple of steps backward while giving the couple a friendly wave, halting when I bump into something. My eyes widen when I spin on my heels to see that I bumped into a some*one,* not a some*thing.*

I instinctively move to steady the woman I've just trampled over like a clumsy ox. "Whoa, there, little lady."

I grip her bare shoulders as she turns her head to look at the monster who almost bowled her over. My chest squeezes as I gaze into the clearest blue eyes I've ever seen. They're the light blue of a cloudless summer day.

I barely have time to take in the wavy blonde hair that tumbles over her shoulders, a little upturned nose, and perfectly formed pink lips before those pretty blue eyes narrow, and she hisses at me venomously, "Watch where you're going!"

I blink, startled at her tone.

She pulls her shoulders from my grip and stomps away, tossing her head like a spirited filly.

I gape after her, my eyes trailing over the long legs revealed by her jean shorts. She's got a tiny waist under the loose white tank top she's wearing, and

those perfectly formed tits ... not to mention her ass
...

*Fuuuck.*

I'm about to go after her to apologize when my phone rings. In the split second it takes to look down at the screen, I lose her. She's nowhere to be seen.

I frown and shake my head as I take the call, scanning the vicinity for any glimpse of her.

It's probably for the best. She looked at me like I was a bug under her shoe, and it's obvious she had a stick up her ass a mile long. I'm the last person she wanted to talk to.

Still, for the rest of the day, I can't get the image of the tiny blonde woman out of my head. When I close my eyes that night, I dream of crystal blue skies framed by thick, dark lashes.

# CHAPTER
# TWO

Emily

MY FACE COLORS with shame when I think of the big cowboy dude from yesterday. I'm never rude like that, but he caught me at a bad moment. I was still stewing over the most recent turn of events with my mother when he backed over me like a dump truck.

Truth be told, I was a bit dazed by his hazel eyes and lightly stubbled jawline—not to mention the way he towered over me, his black cowboy hat, and how he called me "little lady" in that lilting southern drawl. I could tell the man was ripped beneath his button-up shirt. It was all the poor fabric could do to contain those muscles.

I didn't stick around after I hissed at him like a feral cat. At least he doesn't know who I am.

Still, I'm irritated that my thoughts keep drifting back to him, and I have no idea why. He's a stranger, so why does it matter if I was rude to him?

Sitting on the grass by the lake, I try to unwind and enjoy my vacation, yet I can't get the big, hulking stranger out of my mind.

I take in the majestic mountains and the colorful streaks of pink, purple, and amber in the sky. Closing my eyes, I focus on the meditative breathing I learned in yoga class.

Just as my shoulders relax and I start to center, a giggle causes my eyes to snap open. It's a forty-year-old giggle that immediately has all the tension returning to my body.

I look out over the water to see my mother and her ridiculous boy-toy paddle boarding.

I push down the growl that threatens to rumble from my throat. Everywhere I go today, they're there.

They were by the fire pit. They were at the in-ground pool. They were at the volleyball court. Jesus, I can't get away from them. I don't think they're purposefully following me around, but you'd think a resort this size would afford me some peace and quiet away from my mother and her latest fling.

But no, they're present from the moment I wake up,

and if I go out to put some distance between us, they seem to find me. It's making me sick—literally. I lost my appetite at lunch when I saw them finger-feeding each other.

I'm not a shitty daughter who doesn't want her mom to be happy, but I've been through this my entire life. My mom is all hot and heavy for a guy one week, and the next, she's moved on to another. That's why I no longer take the time to learn their names.

My mother goes through men like shoes. She wears them until she's ready for a new style, and then she discards them. It's annoying, especially when her latest pair of shoes is her number one focus while she has them.

Mom has always put me on the back burner. I might as well have raised myself. I'm lucky I had the grades to go to college on a full scholarship because she certainly never put anything aside for my education. She was too busy flitting from man to man. My mom is the definition of "boy crazy."

I hear a loud squeal, and I know it's my mother. Sure enough, a loud splash follows, and I look up to see that her latest fling has dumped her into the water. Her tank top is completely soaked and clinging to her breasts, and it's obvious she's not wearing a bikini underneath.

"Oh, for Christ's sake." I stand with a huff. I don't

know where I'm going, but I need to get far away from my mother. I'm a little more than half her age but twice as mature.

By the time I stop walking, I'm in front of the main lodge. I push my way through the front door, scanning the lobby. Grabbing a disposable cup, I fill my glass with some cucumber water. I take a long sip, enjoying the cool and refreshing flavor when my eyes land on a smattering of business cards on the guest information desk. Scanning them idly, I see one that looks different from the rest. It has a picture of a horse on it. *Horseback riding.*

I pick it up and flick it between my fingers. I've never ridden a horse before, and it might help distract me from my mother and her boy-toy's antics. My mother would never get on a horse, though she'd undoubtedly be a pro with the amount of practice she's had riding things.

I snort at my internal joke.

Taking another sip of the water, I glance at the address. The stable isn't located here at the resort, but it's nearby, which ultimately cements my decision.

I down the rest of my water and pocket the card in my shorts.

Looks like I'm going to learn how to ride a horse.

Anything to get me off this resort and away from my mother's ridiculous giggles.

## Cole

I head up to the office, where my last client of the day waits. My sister shot me a text a few minutes ago to let me know someone signed up for a riding lesson at the last minute.

The woman has never touched a horse, so she's a true beginner.

Completely green beginners are the clients I like to work with the most because I don't have to break them of any bad habits. I can teach her the proper way to approach, saddle, and ride a horse from the get-go.

I'm glad somebody booked another lesson at the last minute. I've been trying to keep busy because every time I go home and close my eyes, I'm haunted by a beauty with blonde hair, blue eyes, and a tongue sharp enough to cut through metal.

I scowl when I realize I'm thinking of her again and shake my head to clear her image from my mind. Taking a deep breath, I push my way through the office door, setting the bell jangling.

And lo-and-behold, the very person I'm trying to get out of my mind is standing right in front of the counter, looking pretty as a picture. I halt in my tracks and stare at her. That blonde hair is waving around her shoulders, and this time she's wearing a red tank top that matches the red fingernail polish on her perfectly manicured nails.

She turns, and those pretty blue eyes assault my senses again.

"What are you doing here, little lady?" The question slips from my lips, unbidden.

Her nose wrinkles in distaste as she glances at me coolly before answering. "Waiting for the riding instructor."

"You're looking at him."

Her eyes widen, and her face flushes. She shakes her head and bites her bottom lip before turning on her heel and heading for the door.

Panic squeezes my chest, and I move in front of the door to block her exit. "Whoa, there. Where are you going?"

She looks at me, and if possible, her face turns an even brighter shade of pink. She squares her shoulders and gives me a pointed look. "We don't have to make this any more awkward than it already is. I didn't know you were the riding instructor. I'm sorry."

I raise an eyebrow at her. "I'm the one who's sorry, darlin'. I never got the chance to properly apologize to you for backing over you the other day."

She worries that puffy bottom lip between her teeth, and I can't stop staring at it, mesmerized. My cock stiffens behind my jeans, and I bite back a groan.

Fuck, she's such a pretty little thing.

"No, I'm sorry," she finally tells me. "I was rude to you. I don't know what came over me. I'm not normally like that."

Her blue eyes are wide when she looks up at me. They're so beautiful, they take my breath away.

I smile and hold out my hand. "So, we're both sorry. We got off on the wrong foot. I'm willing to start over if you are. I'm Cole Montgomery."

She looks at my hand like it's a snake that might bite her before cautiously placing her hand in mine. Our palms touch and I close my hand around hers, marveling at how soft and tiny her hand is.

I resist the urge to tug her flush against my chest. I don't know what this feeling is crashing through me, but my heart is hammering against my ribcage like a stampeding bull, and my blood is rushing through my veins like a bubbling creek.

"Emily Haskins." She tells me in that sweet voice.

"You're not from around here, are you, Emily?"

She arches a delicate eyebrow at me. "What gave me away?"

I grin at her. "Your lack of a southern accent. Where are you from?"

"New York," she says primly.

"Ah, you're a city girl." I'm completely unsurprised by this news. The girl has class written all over her.

"Born and bred, as you say down here."

I smile at her. "So, you want to learn how to ride?" My voice comes out rougher than I intend.

Her face colors, and I realize how that came out a moment too late, but fuck if I'll take it back. I can't keep my eyes from sweeping down her perfect body.

My throat is tight when I add, "A horse, that is. You'd like to learn how to ride a horse."

Her head bobs up and down, her cheeks still flushed. "Yes, I thought I'd try something new."

"Well, you've come to the right place." I grin at her, excited about spending an hour in her presence and learning more about her.

She licks her lips before fluttering those blue eyes at me. "So, you'll teach me?"

"I can teach you darn near anything, darlin'," I drawl, my grin only widening whenever her cheeks turn as red as a tomato. Oh, this is going to be fun.

# CHAPTER
# THREE

Emily

I CAN'T BELIEVE the rugged-looking cowboy I was so rude to is my riding instructor. To his credit, he doesn't seem to hold the incident against me. He apologized for nearly running over me, and now he's leading me over to the stable where tons of enormous beasts are housed. They're so big they tower over me—much like this man.

I swallow, questioning whether I should've signed up to do this.

"Rule number one," Cole's deep voice says. "Horses can sense fear, and if you're skittish, it will make them skittish."

He cuts a knowing glance at me. Maybe he's a horse, too, since he can sense my fear.

I refrain from saying that out loud. We just made good, and I don't want to prove myself to be a humongous bitch again.

"You want to approach a horse confidently yet humbly," he continues. "You want to gain her trust like a dog or any other animal."

Cole walks up to one of the horses sticking its head out of its stall. He pats the horse on the neck before giving her a few strokes while crooning softly to her. He motions to me. "Here, you try. Come pet her."

I take a step back, my eyes wide as I shake my head. "I don't know if I should …" I start to chicken out, but Cole takes my trembling hand in his and tugs me gently toward the horse.

"This is Rosie. She's one of my gentlest mares. She won't bite. I promise." He guides my hand to the horse's white neck as he wraps an arm around my back and pulls me closer. His voice is right next to my ear as he speaks softly. "The trick with any mare is to approach her softly and stroke her right. You want to make her feel safe."

Cole's hot breath fans against my ear as he strokes our hands over the horse's neck. I marvel at the sensation of her hide under my palm and Cole's hand pressed against mine.

He slowly removes his hand until I'm petting the horse on my own, but his heat still surrounds me. I can't contain the huge smile on my face when the horse nickers softly and nuzzles her nose against me. "This is incredible!"

"Yeah," Cole's deep voice agrees.

I chance a glance at him, and he's looking at me, not the horse. A blush overtakes me, but I clear my throat and look away. "Okay, so now what? When do I ride her?"

Cole chuckles. It's a rumbling sound that bubbles up from his chest. "Whoa, don't get ahead of yourself there, darlin'. Today, you're just going to get to know her, and I'll teach you the basics about horses. We won't mount her until tomorrow."

There's a gruff note to his voice when he says that. I look at him curiously, but he clears his throat and starts teaching me about the equipment and giving me a run-down of the horses.

Cole's voice is so soothing. It washes over the horses and me. He has such a deep timbre. I could listen to it all day. No wonder the horses are so relaxed around him.

He removes the saddle after showing me how to put it on. "You won't have to worry about this," he tells me. "I'll saddle the mare for you tomorrow, but I always like to show people how to do it themselves."

I watch him as he swaggers to the corner to hang up the saddle, noticing how perfectly those jeans hug his ass.

My cheeks color when he turns around, and I see the large bulge in the front of his jeans. My eyes quickly dart away from him. My cheeks flame and I look anywhere but at the huge man towering over me.

"Who are you on vacation with?" he asks me casually.

"How do you know I didn't come alone?"

Cole pauses before he answers. "Because pretty young women don't usually travel alone. They come in packs, so I'm guessing you're here with friends."

I raise an eyebrow at him. "Maybe I'm vacationing with my husband."

His eyes flash. "No man in his right mind would let you out of his sight for a second."

My breath hitches in my throat. His hazel eyes bore into mine, holding me captive. I finally tear my gaze from him. "This was supposed to be a mother-daughter vacation," I say with a bitter laugh.

Cole says nothing but raises an eyebrow.

"She ditched me for her boyfriend." I leave it at that, not wanting to get into the sorry details. That's a sure way to ruin my mood.

He nods. "Are you and your mother close?"

"Not even remotely," I admit.

If he thinks it's strange we're not close, he doesn't comment on it. Instead, he tactfully changes the subject. "So, you're from the city. What do you do up there?"

"I'm in advertising."

He whistles under his breath.

"What about you?" I peek at him as I continue to stroke Rosie. "Have you ever lived in the city?"

He laughs a deep, booming laugh like I've said something hilariously funny. "Me? Hell, no, darlin'. I hate the city. I need fresh air to keep me sane."

I admire how his chest muscles flex against his shirt when he laughs. He notices me watching him and sobers. My breath catches as we gaze at one another. He stares at me intensely, like he's trying to see into my soul.

"Do you want to get a bite to eat?" He finally breaks the silence.

"Oh." I bite my lip as I hesitate. This man and I are polar opposites, and I made a terrible first impression on him, but he seems to have easily forgiven me.

"I promise I won't bite Emily—or step on you again," he adds with a hint of a smile.

I laugh and hear myself agreeing. "Sure, why not?"

Cole

EMILY HASKINS ENCHANTS ME. This beautiful city girl has my country heart wrapped around her little finger, and she doesn't even know it.

She agreed to have dinner with me, and even though she's dressed casually in jean shorts and a red tank top, she conducts herself with class. She might as well be wearing a long evening gown. She moves so fluidly. Everything about her is graceful. I'm not a romantic man, but she's poetry in motion. Like the sun, she shines so brightly it almost hurts to look directly at her.

Me, on the other hand? I'm unpolished and underdressed. The restaurant I brought her to isn't a super fancy joint, but it's not a hole-in-the-wall diner either. I look precisely what I am—an undeserving country boy with dirty jeans who stinks like a stable, yet this gorgeous woman is laughing at every stupid joke I crack.

She's so different from the woman who hissed at me like a viper that first day. I see now that had something to do with her mother pulling some shady shit. She led Emily to believe she wanted to spend time with her, but her boyfriend conveniently turned up at the resort.

It's clear Emily doesn't want to talk about her mother, so I listen as she talks about her job. I love the way her eyes glow with passion when she speaks about what she does. It's obvious she loves it.

I can relate. I feel the same way about working with horses.

"I'm a bit of a workaholic," she finally admits. "This is the first vacation I've ever taken."

I raise an eyebrow at that. "What about all work and no play?"

She shrugs and lets out a self-deprecating laugh. "I am rather dull."

Denial crashes through me like a freight train, and I reach across the table to grab her hands. "You are not dull, darlin'. You're brighter than the sun on an August morn."

She blinks before she laughs teasingly. "Are you sure you're not a writer in your spare time? You certainly have a way with words, Mr. Montgomery."

"Cole," I correct her.

"What?"

"Call me Cole." My voice comes out husky, but I'm dying to hear her say my name. "I need to hear what my name sounds like in that pretty voice before this night is through."

"I think I need to be getting back, Cole." Her voice is shaky and breathless.

My cock responds to the sound of my name on her lips. It swells to full mast and presses against the zipper of my jeans. She's shut the night down, but she said my name, so I'll take it as a victory.

I throw some money on the table to cover the check. "Here, let me walk you to your cabin."

"Oh, that's okay. You don't have to."

"I know I don't have to, darlin', but I want to."

She bites that damn lip again, and it's enough to drive me crazy. I want to bite it myself and see how her lips taste. I already know she's going to be sweet as sugar.

We walk in a charged silence, me holding her hand like I'll never let go. I might not.

When we get to her cabin, her mother is sitting on the porch with her supposed boyfriend. They're laughing and kissing and humping all over each other like horny teenagers.

Emily's countenance instantly sours. "Jesus," she mutters, her face turning scarlet. "I'm sorry about this. My mother is worse than a teenager."

I smile at her reassuringly. "I'll see you tomorrow morning."

"Yes." She returns my smile. "I can't wait. I'm eager to see what it feels like."

My mind takes that statement and runs in a thousand directions with it—all of them sexual.

"To ride the horse, I mean. I can't wait to see what it feels like to ride a horse," she rushes to add.

Her face is flushed so prettily, and I decide that making Emily blush will be my new life mission.

I lean down until my lips are only an inch from hers, and I fist my hands at my sides to keep from dragging her to me and kissing her in front of her mother.

"Goodnight, Emily."

It takes every ounce of self-control I have to straighten and walk away from her, but I don't want our first kiss to be marred by anything.

*Tomorrow, Emily, I'm going to give you the ride of your life.*

———

I'm so eager to see Emily again that I can't wait for her to come to the stables, so I wait outside her cabin bright and early the following morning.

I look like a psycho showing up uninvited like this, but when she steps out onto the porch in a pair of little jean shorts that show off those magnificent legs and a white tank top, my body starts doing funny things. My heart rate ticks up. My breathing becomes erratic. My nostrils flare.

And when those pretty blue eyes meet mine, I swear to God, I see my entire world in them.

I replayed every moment of yesterday back in my mind before falling asleep last night, and when I did sleep, I dreamed of those cloudless, sky-blue eyes.

I'm obsessed with Emily Haskins.

"Cole!" She says my name in surprise.

My dick rises to attention. Fuck, how can my name on her lips make my cock hard like this? I'd probably cream in my pants if I ever got a flash of one of her tits or her sweet pussy.

"What are you doing here?" she asks as she comes skipping down the porch steps.

I try to play it cool. "I was in the neighborhood and thought I'd give you a ride over to the stable so you don't have to take a taxi or walk."

She smiles at me. "That's incredibly thoughtful of you, but you didn't have to do that. Thank you."

If she only knew I'm doing this for entirely selfish reasons because I thought I'd die if I didn't lay eyes on her again soon. "Have you eaten yet?"

She holds up a banana, and my throat goes dry. I walk her over to my truck, where I hold the door open for her and buckle her up.

She looks at me strangely as I hop into the driver's side of my four-wheel drive.

"What is it, darlin'?"

"No one has ever buckled me up like that before."

"I don't know what kind of men you've been hanging out with in New York City, but they're not gentlemen if they don't properly see to your safety." I tighten my hands on the steering wheel at the thought of her going out with other men.

She considers that before she confesses, "That's probably it. I don't hang out with many men."

I exhale a breath. Yep, that explains it. This woman is an admitted workaholic, and that's the only reason some lucky bastard hasn't snatched her up yet because, on a scale of one to ten, she's a million.

Emily peels open the banana, and my throat works as I swallow, trying not to look as she takes a bite of the phallic fruit. My motherfucking dick turns to steel in my pants. The fucker is leaking, and I bite the inside of my cheek to keep from groaning.

And here's the thing. I know Emily isn't doing this on purpose. She has no idea what the sight of her eating that fucking banana does to me. I innately know this, and it's a testament to the depth of my depravity because knowing she's *that* sweet and innocent turns me on even more.

It's a short drive over to the stables from the resort, and thankfully, she's finished eating the banana by the time I throw my truck into park. She jumps out of the truck with a little hop before I can get around to her side to help her down. She looks so young when she does it, which gives me pause.

"How old are you, darlin'?"

She cocks her head to the side before she answers. "Twenty-two. Why do you ask?"

"Standard procedure. I need to know your age before taking you out on the horse," I lie.

"What about you?" she asks.

My lips quirk into a grin as I hook my thumbs in my belt loops. "How old do I look?"

She chews on her lip as she studies my face before pronouncing confidently, "Thirty-five."

I feign hurt. "I'll have you know I'm thirty-four, little lady."

She doesn't miss a beat. "When do you turn thirty-five?"

"In a month," I admit begrudgingly.

She laughs, and the sound is like music to my ears.

Christ, I'm thirteen years older than this woman. I've got no business thinking the thoughts I do when I look at her tight, young body.

Tell that to my cock.

"You ready to do this?" I ask, trying to get my mind out of the gutter.

She nods her head enthusiastically.

I lead her over to the stable, where I let her get reacquainted with Rosie while I saddle her up. When Rosie is all ready to go, I don't give Emily the option to mount her on her own. Partly because I know she's way too short to manage it without a stepladder, but also because I'm greedy and want any opportunity to touch her.

Emily lets out a yelp when I clasp my hands around her waist and lift her effortlessly onto the mare's back. She grips the saddle with wide eyes and a huge smile on her face. My chest feels tight. Fuck, she's so beautiful when she smiles like that.

"Wow," she breathes.

I grin at her excitement. "You ain't seen nothing yet, darlin'. Wait 'til we get to movin'."

I see the questions in her eyes when I say "we," but

I don't give her a chance to voice them before sliding into the saddle behind her. This is completely unorthodox. I never ride with my trainees, but I'll take any excuse to get closer to Emily.

And holy fuck, she feels amazing. I wrap my arms around her and grab the reins. Emily is so tiny the top of her head barely reaches my chin. I inhale deeply, flooding my senses with the floral scent of her shampoo. She smells good enough to eat, and my cock swells even harder in my jeans. If the fucker keeps going, he's going to rip clean through them.

"What now?" Emily asks, her voice breathless.

Is she overwhelmed riding a horse for the first time? Or is it the proximity of our bodies causing that breathlessness? Having her in my arms is overwhelming in all the best ways, and I will not take one moment of this for granted.

"Now we ride."

# CHAPTER
# FIVE

Emily

I'VE NEVER HAD butterflies before, but when Cole's arms wrap around me, caging me in bands of hard, corded muscle, it feels like a thousand tiny wings have taken flight right behind my belly button.

We're sitting so close that I can feel the heat from his chest emanating through my clothes and seeping into my back. I sit up straight, so I'm not leaning against him like a desperate hussy.

Cole's voice is a deep rumble in my ear as he shows me how to hold the reins and turn the horse. "Here, you try."

His hands drop from the reins, leaving me in charge

of the horse. I don't know what I do, and the horse takes off. It's so sudden that I slam against the hard wall of Cole's chest.

"Whoa!" He's quick to grab the reins and soothe the horse, stroking her neck calmly.

My heart is about to beat out of my chest. The way the horse shot off and the burning brick wall of Cole's chest behind me have me flustered. I might be a virgin, but something suspiciously large is pressing against my ass through our jeans.

"I'm sorry." I lean forward and try to wiggle away.

Cole wraps an arm around my waist and holds me still. "Stop wiggling, woman," he breathes harshly.

I freeze, my face coloring as I realize what's going on. My God, *I* made him hard. Cole's ragged breaths are fanning over my hair, and a rush of feminine power crashes through me at the knowledge that *I'm* the one who has him so worked up.

My breath becomes shallow, and my clit throbs. The overwhelming sensation of Cole's nearness mixed with my newly instilled fear after the horse's flight makes me dizzy.

"I think I'm ready to get off," I tell Cole breathlessly.

"Fuck, me too," he growls.

My cheeks flame when I realize we mean those

words in entirely different ways. "The horse, Cole. I'm ready to get off the horse."

He swings his leg off the horse in one fluid motion and then grabs me by the waist and lifts me from the saddle. My body slides against his as he lowers me to the ground, and I can feel every sculpted ridge of muscle before he plants me on my feet.

His hazel eyes burn into mine beneath the brim of his black cowboy hat. I tremble, and his nostrils flare like a bull preparing to charge.

"Fuck, darlin'," he growls, wrapping his hand around the nape of my neck and crushing his lips to mine. He pulls my body flush against him as he devours my mouth like a starving man.

He thrusts his hips against me, and the raging column of his flesh presses into my stomach through his jeans. I whimper at how big he feels. I'm not a total innocent. I've read plenty of romance novels and even watched a bit of porn just to satiate my curiosity, so I know Cole is hung like a horse. I also know that what he's packing between his legs will destroy a virgin pussy like mine. That should scare me, so why do I feel an answering throb between my legs?

"You taste sweeter than apple pie, Emily," he murmurs before taking my mouth in another deep kiss.

Holy moly, I've been kissed before, but never like

this. This man kisses me like it's the end of the world, and I'm the only thing that will save him.

"You know I haven't been able to stop thinking about you from the moment I first saw you," he breathes as he trails kisses along my jaw and down my throat.

The admission throws me because I haven't been able to stop thinking about him either. "I was so rude to you."

He chuckles. "You were so pretty when you were ripping me a new asshole. You looked like a little hellcat with your eyes flashing fire and your claws out. No woman has ever spoken to me that way before."

I don't imagine they have. They were probably too busy falling over themselves, trying to get in line for some of these kisses.

Cole slides his hands over my shoulders and tugs my tank top down to reveal my breasts. A shudder goes through him as he looks down at them lustfully. My nipples are painfully hard, and my breath comes in short pants as I wait for him to take one into his mouth. I've never felt a man's mouth on my nipples before, but my hardened pebbles are aching for the touch of his mouth and tongue.

He stands there staring down at them with a glazed look in his eye.

"Cole?" I ask uncertainly. "Are you okay?"

"No," he grits out. "I'm trying my best not to jizz in my pants just looking at these perfect little titties."

The cords of his neck are taut, and his head rolls back when I wiggle in his arms. He groans and tightens his arm around me to hold me still. "You're enough to make a man embarrass himself, Emily."

The way he grunts out those words is so hot my knees go weak. I whimper, and suddenly I can't help myself. I rub my nipples back and forth against his shirt, seeking any sort of friction.

He groans deep in his throat before he drops his head and finally captures my breast in his hot, wet mouth, suckling it deep. I loop my arms around his neck, knocking his cowboy hat off in the process. He doesn't seem to mind, and I certainly don't as I spear my fingers into his thick, sandy locks.

"You want a ride, darlin'? I'll give you one. Right here on this big dick." His voice is deep and gravelly, and God, what his growls and rasps do to me.

I hear him unzipping his pants, and then he's undoing my shorts and yanking them and my panties down my legs in one swoop.

I barely have time to look down at the monster he's fisting in his hands before he lifts me in his arms. My legs wrap around him instinctively, and I feel the bulbous crown of his cock prodding at my entrance.

Another shudder passes through him. "Fuck, Emily.

That sweet little thing is so wet for me. You need my cock, don't you, darlin'?"

His filthy words set me aflame. My head falls back, and I moan by way of answer, but he's having none of that.

He grabs my neck and forces me to meet his eyes. "If you don't want this, now's the time to speak up, darlin', because once I bust that little pussy wide open, I don't think I'll be able to stop."

I bite my lip and feel my pussy clench around air in response to his words. Cole's hazel eyes flick down to my lips as he growls in the back of his throat. His chest heaves as he tears his gaze from them to my eyes.

"Emily." His voice is ragged, desperate, "You're killing me here. Tell me you want this."

I only hesitate a moment longer. "Yes."

The word is barely out of my mouth before Cole slams himself up into me. I scream as he punches his way through my hymen. I cling to him, shuddering and gasping, dragging in little panting breaths through my mouth as I struggle to adjust to the sudden fullness of him inside me.

"Fuuuck," he groans out long and deep. "How the fuck are you so tight? So tight. Fuck! So tight."

As if it's just dawned on him, he goes completely still. He pulls back to look down between us and sees the blood that's no doubt staining his cock.

His eyes are wide when he looks back up at me, whispering in a mixture of horror and fascination, "You're a virgin?"

I flush at his tone. "Is that bad?"

He lets out a strangled breath, and I feel him twitch inside me. "No, darlin', it's the most beautiful gift anyone has ever given me. I'm floored that you let me be your first." His voice drops a notch as he pushes up inside me. He strokes against my inner walls and growls, "I'm going to be your only too. This pussy is officially mine."

God help me, but his possessive growls have me involuntarily clenching around him. He feels it because his eyes take on a feral gleam. He ruts into me harder and deeper and faster.

"You like that, don't you, darlin'. You got me locked down over this pussy. I'm barely inside you, and you got me thinking about giving you my last name and every dollar I own."

I don't even have time to process the magnitude of what he just said because he stabs this spot deep inside me that causes me to see stars, and then I can't help myself. I throw myself back down on him, needing to feel more of that delicious sensation.

"Fuck yes, darlin'," he growls. "Ride that cock. This pussy needs a ride, you bring it right here to me. You hear me, little lady?"

I don't know if he expects an answer, but I'm beyond speaking. I'm lost in sensation as every nerve ending in my body snaps while he slides in and out of me.  His big arms envelop me, and I savor his grunts and growls and groans in my ear.

Something is building inside me. It's something monumental that I know will change my life forever.

"Cole!" His name comes out as a plea, but I don't know what I'm begging for, just that whatever it is, he's the one who can give it to me.

"I know, darlin'. I know," he croons at me soothingly. "I'm right there with you. We'll jump off that cliff together." His breathing becomes ragged. "You ready, little lady? Huh?"

"Yes!"

He grunts. "Here we go! Come with me!"

As if those words were the permission I was waiting for, my entire body spasms with my release. It's so intense I can't even make a sound. My mouth falls open into a silent "o" as I convulse around Cole's throbbing flesh.

Cole, on the other hand, is louder than ever. He roars like a big bull, and then I feel his hot heat spurting up inside me. It's the most incredible feeling, and it sends new waves of pleasure crashing over me. I cling to him, my arms and legs wrapped around him as my entire body shakes.

I don't know how long Cole holds me, but he's still twitching inside me several minutes later. My inner thighs are soaked with our combined juices when he finally pulls out.

He pulls my panties and shorts up and buttons them with utmost care before adjusting my tank top and placing a tender kiss on my lips. He tucks himself back in his pants before sitting with his back against a nearby tree and pulling me into his lap.

His cum is still inside me, and I never thought it would be sexy to have a man's release dripping out of me, but it is.

My limbs feel heavy, and I lay my head on Cole's chest, more content than I've ever been. There's no awkwardness, just a pulsing warmth flowing between us. It's something I can't explain. We don't speak because no words could do it justice.

I close my eyes and breathe in Cole's scent. It's something spicy, woodsy, and outdoorsy. It's incredible, and I could get high off it.

"Is that included in all your horseback riding lessons?" I ask him playfully.

Cole's chest rumbles under my ear like a big bear. "Only for you, little darlin'."

I smile, and before I know it, the gentle rise and fall of his chest lulls me to sleep.

# CHAPTER
# SIX

Emily

I DON'T GO BACK to my cabin that night. Cole swings me back up on the horse before jumping on behind me and wrapping his arms around me. He pulls me close to him so I can feel his chest pressed right against my back.

He takes us back to the stables, where I help him brush down Rosie and put everything up. Then we hop in his truck, and he takes us to his home, a quaint, secluded cabin in the middle of the mountains.

I'm in awe of how peaceful and serene it looks. "It's so beautiful," I tell him as I take in the wooded area.

"Yes," he agrees with me, but he's looking at me and not the cabin.

Cole's eyes darken, and my heart does a flip. He takes my hand and leads me up the porch and into his house, where he promptly strips off his shirt.

My mouth goes dry at all the naked muscle in front of me. Good Lord. I knew he was ripped from having him pressed against me, but nothing could have prepared my eyes for the visual of his bare chest. Cole is a rugged masterpiece. Plain and simple. He has a warrior's chest.

His eyes light with pleasure when he sees me staring at him. "Come here, darlin'." His voice is husky, and he doesn't give me a chance to obey him before he grabs my hand and pulls me to him, roping his arms around me and effectively caging me in.

His swollen cock strains against his pants, making his intentions clear. He takes my mouth in a gentle kiss, this one less hurried than the one before.

"Our first time was rough, but now I'm going to take my time with you and worship you like the goddess you are."

His words set my knees trembling, and I'm afraid I'm going to collapse into a puddle of goo at his feet. Hoisting me into his arms, he carries me into the bathroom, where he sets me gently on my feet and turns on the shower.

He undresses me slowly, taking his time as his hands slide over my skin. Shucking out of his clothes, he takes my hand and guides me into the shower.

The moment is like something sacred. He doesn't speak as he washes every inch of my body, lingering over my breasts and between my thighs. He's rock hard, but he ignores his erection as he makes quick work of washing himself.

He dries me off with the utmost care when we're both clean before quickly drying himself and carrying me to bed.

True to his word, he worships me. His lips don't leave one inch of my skin untouched, and when he kisses me in that most intimate of places where no one has ever kissed me before, I turn into a sobbing, blabbering mess.

My fingers grip the damp strands of his hair as I beg and plead with him for release.

He thrashes his tongue furiously over my swollen clit, and I shatter into a million tiny pieces, screaming his name. He growls as he continues to eat me through my orgasm.

When I'm lying completely lax, he crawls on top of me, a heated look in his eyes. "Feeling you come on my face is the single most euphoric experience of my life," he tells me, kissing me ardently. I taste myself on him, which makes the experience much more erotic.

He pushes into me slowly, feeding me inch after precious inch of his thickness until I'm so full I could burst.

"Fuck, Emily, I've never felt anything like you in my entire life," he tells me as he holds himself inside me.

He kisses my forehead so tenderly that it makes my heart swell with emotion. How can I feel so much for this man I just met?

As if his thoughts mirror mine, he whispers, "You complete me, Emily Haskins. I don't care if it's fast. You're mine now, darlin', and I'm never letting you go."

Why does my soul thrill at those words?

I can't answer him, so I turn my lips to meet his kiss.

He fucks me and makes love to me in turns all night long. I'm the least rested I've been since I got here, yet I'm glowing and happier than I can ever remember.

Cole only agrees to release me because he has other classes booked. "I'll be right back here to get your sweet ass as soon as I'm done with work, darlin'," he tells me, punctuating his words with a heated kiss. "Grab all your bags because you're staying with me from now on," he adds as I jump out of his truck.

He watches to make sure I get inside okay before he backs his truck out of the driveway and leaves.

I'm still smiling dreamily when my mother's shrill voice cuts through my daydream. "You didn't come back last night."

I turn to where she's standing in the living room with her arms crossed, frowning at me. I shake my head with a bemused grin on my face. Is she serious? She waits until I'm twenty-two years old to care about how late I stay out?

"I'm surprised you noticed at all. Aren't you busy with What's-His-Name? Or have you already moved on to someone else?" I say it half-teasingly, half-seriously.

My mom doesn't even wince. She looks at me evenly. "You shouldn't get involved with him. You barely know him."

My mouth drops open as I stare at her incredulously. "Wow, Mom. Talk about the pot calling the kettle black." When she continues to stare at me sternly, I let out a disbelieving laugh. "Are you serious right now?"

"I know what I'm talking about, Emily," she insists.

I'm shocked we're even having this conversation. I don't think my mother has ever spoken to me in such a stern tone before, and I'm mind-boggled about the entire thing.

It's fucking with my head, and all the pent-up frustration I've suppressed over the years finally comes bubbling out. "No. You don't get to do this right now." I motion between us. "You don't get to play the caring mother. Not now I've grown up. You certainly don't get to give me advice about men. Not when you're the biggest slut I know."

Again, my mom doesn't even blink. She stands there with her lips pursed before she finally says, "That's fair. But let me tell you this, Emily. There's a reason I don't get too attached to a man."

She pauses as if she expects me to ask her why, but I just cross my arms and glare at her.

"When you keep a man around for too long, you risk catching feelings for him, and then he'll do nothing but use you. I learned that the hard way. It's best to play with them and put them back before they get the chance."

Something about my mother's words and her weary tone of voice gives me pause. She sounds so lonely—my mother, who's never lacking for male companionship. I stare at her sadly, wondering who hurt her enough to have her believe this is the way it should be.

"I just don't want to see you get hurt, Em." Mom's voice is soft when she calls me by my nickname. "You remind me so much of myself when I was your age, with stars and dreams in your eyes." She smiles sadly as she looks at me. "You've got that dangerous look in your eyes."

I frown. "What do you mean?"

"You're falling in love." Her eyes are sympathetic before she reminds me gently, "And you know this can never work. Your man is a country boy, through and through. I've seen him swaggering around the resort with that walk that says he was born in the saddle. You're a city girl, Em. You're here on vacation, and he knows that. You're nothing but a fling to him."

Mom's words cut deep because it's what I've been afraid of deep down, too.

*But Cole said you were his. Remember the possessive way he claimed you and said he's never letting you go?*

*Words spoken in passion*, my rational mind reminds me.

"Emily, I know you think I'm a total flake, and I know I've not been the best mother, but I'm only trying to help you, not hurt you, honey."

I stare at this woman who's my mother but not. She's right. She hasn't been the best mother, but I know she's right. There's no way Cole and I can ever be more than a fling.

I don't say another word. I go to my room and begin packing up my things, my heart heavy with what I know I have to do.

Cole

I HUM A TUNE, my heart lighter than it's ever been. I love my job, but I couldn't wait for the day to end so I could have Emily back in my arms again. I've been jonesing for her all day, like a junkie needing his next hit.

I take the steps up to her cabin two at a time in my haste to see her. I recognize the woman who answers my knock as Emily's mother and greet her with a respectful, "Good evening, Miss Haskins. I'm here for Emily."

"Em's not here," the woman tells me coolly.

I blink at her tone, wondering what crawled up her

craw. "Okay, where can I find her? Did she go up to the main lodge?"

The woman gives me an assessing glance. "Look, Mister...?"

"Cole," I tell her. "You can call me Cole."

"Cole." She nods. "Emily went back to New York."

My heart falls to my feet, and blood rushes in my ears. *"What?"*

The woman blinks. She looks taken aback before she schools her features and shrugs. "Look at it this way. You don't have the awkwardness of ending your fling now."

I glare at her. "Emily is not a fling. She's everything to me."

Emily's mom snorts. "Yeah, you're in love with her after what? Two days?"

My heart hammers against my rib cage. I don't have time to explain myself to this woman. I need to find *my* woman. "Where can I find her in New York?"

Ms. Haskins blinks again before she sniffs and asks, "And why should I tell you that? So you can go up there and break her heart whenever you decide you're done with her?"

I study Emily's mother in a new light. I see the old pain hiding behind her eyes and realize she's speaking from experience. I work to keep my voice gentle when I tell her honestly, "I would never hurt Emily. I know it seems fast, but I am in love with your daughter, ma'am. The first time I looked into her pretty blue eyes, I was a goner. Call it love at first sight. Call it obsession. I don't care what the fuck you call it. All I know is I feel like I'll die if I don't see her again soon. So, you can help me out, or I'll have to waste a bunch of time searching every motherfucking inch of New York City to find her. But make no mistake, I will *not* stop until I do."

Ms. Haskins' eyes are brimming with tears at the end of my speech. She covers her mouth with her hand before she nods and then rattles off an address.

I grab her hand and kiss the back of it before I swear to her, "You won't regret helping me. I promise you."

She nods and gives me a watery smile before warning, "You better not hurt her."

"Never," I vow to her and myself.

I hop in my truck and call my sister, telling her to cancel all my appointments for the upcoming week.

I drive as fast as I can to catch the next flight to New York.

*I'm coming, darlin'.*

———

Emily

. . .

I sit alone in my apartment, wallowing in self-pity and eating strawberry ice cream straight from the tub like they do on those cheesy rom-coms when a girl goes through a breakup. It always makes the girl feel better, but it's not working for me. It's a good thing the ice cream melts in my mouth because I don't have the energy to chew.

I put the tub back in the freezer, abandoning my effort to eat my emotions away. It doesn't work. Some girls can eat their way through the tears, but not me. I lose my appetite and have to starve my way through my emotional turmoil.

Tears spring to my eyes when the cowboy on the screen calls the Southern belle "little lady."

Yeah, I suddenly have a penchant for old western movies. So shoot me. It has absolutely nothing to do with the heroes reminding me of a certain horseback riding instructor from Virginia. Nope, nothing at all.

Fresh tears sting my eyes. I'm such a liar. It has everything to do with him.

My mother is right—something I never would have believed. I've been foolish. I only knew Cole for two days, and look at me. I'm crying like we were in a fifteen-year relationship. I'm such an idiot. I'm sure he's moved on without me.

I wish I could go back to work, but I still have vacation time. I curse myself for agreeing to take the vacation in the first place. My mother bailed on me and then did a complete one-eighty by acting like the concerned mother. It's a wonder I don't have whiplash.

I sniff and wipe my eyes when I hear a knock at my door. I sigh. The only person who knocks on my door is my next-door neighbor when he's run out of Earl Grey and wants to borrow some from me. I'm not in the mood to chat with old Mr. Peterson, but I trudge to the door anyway. I'll let him borrow whatever he needs and tell him I'm going to bed.

My eyes widen when I open the door. It's not Mr. Peterson.

"Cole?"

His hazel eyes blaze down at me. "Emily."

He removes the hat and shifts on his feet as he holds it in front of him. His sandy hair looks disheveled like he's run his fingers through it a bunch of times.

I stand there staring at him in shock.

"Can I come in?"

His deep voice rocks me to my core, and I bite my lip before I step back to let him in.

"What are you—?" I don't get to finish my question because he grabs my face and kisses me ardently.

My heart starts pitter-pattering into overdrive as my hands find purchase against his hard chest.

"What do you mean, what am I doing here, darlin'?" he growls. "The question is, what are *you* doing here?"

My brow furrows in confusion. "I live here."

He scoffs. "I know, little lady. I mean, why did you come back without telling me?"

I shake my head and push away from him. His frown deepens with every step I take back from him, but I need the distance to keep my head clear for what I'm about to say. I lick my lips nervously. "What we had was nice, Cole, but it was never going to last. I'm a city girl, and you hate the city."

Cole makes an animalistic sound. "Is that you or your mother talking?"

My mouth falls open as I stare at him.

"Is that what this is about?" he goes on.

"I—"

"Am I just a fling to you?" He cuts me off.

"What?" I sputter. "I…I…that's what I am to you!" Pain pierces my heart at speaking the truth out loud.

He grabs me and pulls me to him, and a growl rumbles in his chest. "Where in the world did you get that idea, little lady? Did you not hear me when I laid my heart on the floor at your feet? What did you think

I meant when I said you were mine and I was never letting you go, woman?"

My heart beats erratically as Cole stares at me, waiting for an answer. I lick my lips, and his eyes darken. "I don't know," I finally whisper. "I thought you were just saying it in the heat of the moment."

"Bullshit," he snaps. "Don't lie to me and tell me you don't feel this insane connection pulsing between us like a live wire. And know this, Emily." He grabs my face between his hands and looks directly into my eyes, searing me with his intensity. "I will never tell you anything I don't mean, so when I said I was keeping you, that's exactly what I intend to do, woman."

My heart melts, but then my eyes fall on his black cowboy hat discarded on the floor. "We live in two different worlds, Cole."

"No, we don't," he tells me adamantly. "Not anymore. Because the only world I want to live in is the one where I have you. If that's in the city, then sign me up."

Tears gather in my eyes. "You would do that for me? Leave the country that you love so much?"

"Emily, darlin'. I would do anything for you. Nothing is more important to me than you. When I looked into your pretty blue eyes, I saw my entire world. You're all I'll ever need, and if you want to live in the city, then that's where we'll live. I don't care where we go. I don't care what we do—so long as we're together. Don't ever run away from me like that again, woman," he growls before smashing his lips onto mine and kissing me possessively.

Our chests are heaving when he finally pulls back and rests his forehead against mine. "What's going on in that pretty head of yours?" he asks as he strokes his thumb along my cheek.

I smile and let out a laugh. "I missed my last riding lesson with you."

His lips tip up in a devastatingly handsome grin as he drawls, "Don't worry, darlin'. I'll give you as many rides as you want for the rest of our lives." He falls onto my couch and pulls me down, so I'm sitting astride him. "Starting now." He grins at me wickedly before kissing me again.

I melt into him. Cole and I might be opposites, but he completes me.

I feel that hard part of him jutting up against my stomach and reach down between us to cup him through his jeans.

He hisses in a sharp breath and thrusts his hips against my hand. "Fuck, Emily, darlin'. Do you have any idea what you do to me, little lady?"

Before I can answer, Cole lifts me and yanks my shorts and panties down in one swoop. His chest heaves up and down urgently as he hurries to unleash his cock from his jeans.

It bobs up between us, tall and proud, and he positions me on top of him. "Get ready for the ride of your life, darlin'."

"Cole!" I gasp out his name as he impales me on his huge girth.

He slaps my ass as he bottoms out inside me. My instincts take over, and I ride him. He holds my ass in both hands and helps bounce me up and down on him. "Yes, darlin'," he encourages me. "You're doing so good. Get it, honey. It's yours. Only yours."

His words warm my heart and send fire racing through my veins. I feel more moisture pooling between my thighs as electricity crackles through me where we're connected. I squeeze around him involuntarily, and Cole groans before smashing his lips onto mine.

He kisses me possessively, growling into my mouth. "Don't you ever run from me like that again. You hear me?" he rasps against my lips as I continue to ride him, the pressure within me building, building. It's all I can focus on. "Emily." His voice cracks across me like a whip, breaking through my haze of lust and drawing my attention back to his eyes. "I love you, darlin'."

I soften, a tingle snapping through me as he thrusts

up and hits a spot inside me that makes me see stars. "I love you too."

His hands move from my ass to my hips. He holds me still as he jabs up into me rapidly. I can't catch my breath. The pleasure is so intense, and I know my orgasm is near. It's right there. I can almost feel it.

"Who do you belong to?"

I can't talk. All I can do is cling to him.

He slows down, and I whimper in protest.

"Who?" he prompts.

"You!" I scream in frustration. "Cole!" My desperate plea must break through to him because he gives me what I want and finishes me off with a few more perfect upward thrusts of his hips.

I scream his name again, my world falling apart around me.

"Motherfucker, Emily!" he curses.

I feel his hot release jetting up into me, and it causes me to convulse around him again. Seeing him lose control like this heightens my own pleasure.

I come so hard it's like I temporarily leave my body. When I come back to my senses, Cole is stroking his hands along my back.

"I'm glad you came for me." I smile against his neck.

"I'll always come for you," he says, his voice filled with innuendo.

I swat his shoulder. "You know what I mean."

He sobers and tilts my chin to capture my eyes with his own. "Yes, and I mean it that way too. I'll always come for you. You're my everything, Emily. Nothing else in my life matters without you."

# EPILOGUE

*Two Years Later*

Cole

I COME up behind my wife and wrap my arms around her, cupping her pregnant belly. Emily and I have been married a little over a year, and we live in my cabin. I was serious when I told her I would move to the city with her if that's what she wanted, but she did some negotiating at the firm she works for, and my woman is so good at what she does that the company was willing to let her work remotely.

She does her job virtually, only flying into the city when she has to, and I'm right by her side when she does because I can't bear to let her out of my sight for long.

Emily and her mother are back on speaking terms again, and I daresay they're growing a bit closer all the time. Emily can't forget that her mother was absent growing up, but I think she understands why her mother is the way she is when it comes to men. The woman had her heart broken, plain and simple. I'm just glad that Emily didn't stick to her mother's advice that day and keep me at a distance. I don't know what I'd have done if she'd rejected me when I went after her.

Actually, yeah, I do. I would have picked her up, thrown her over my shoulder, and brought her back with me anyway. Because she's my woman, and we belong together. It's that simple.

I kiss her neck, and she places her little hands atop mine as she leans against me. I love it when she leans into me like this, so trustingly. "You about done here, darlin'?"

"That depends." I hear the smile in her voice. "Are you offering me a ride?" She turns in my arms and smiles at me coyly.

My cock jumps in my jeans at the thought of

sheathing myself in her tight heat. "You know what I told you. You can hop on me anytime, darlin'."

She smiles radiantly and pushes me into the chair. Dropping to her knees before me, she unzips me, holding my eyes the entire time. My cock bobs in the air between us, thick and heavy. Precum is already dribbling from the slit, and I moan as she wraps her hands around the base.

She places a gentle, teasing kiss on the head before she swirls her tongue around it, licking up the moisture there and moaning in the back of her throat. I grip the arms of the chair tightly as I try to sit still and take what she gives me, but fuck, it's all I can do not to come down her throat when she keeps holding eye contact with me and plunges her mouth down on my dick.

When she deep-throats me, my eyes roll back in my head. I grab her hair with a muffled curse, yanking her off me, and my cock falls from her mouth with a wet pop.

"You better jump up on this dick right now, little lady," I tell her sternly.

Lust lights her eyes as she slips her panties off beneath the little maternity dress she's wearing and scrambles on top of me. We groan in unison as her hot heat slides down on me. I'm splitting her pussy wide open, and she struggles to take me all the way in. I help her by holding on to her hips and thrusting hard and deep until I'm fully seated inside her.

Her head falls back on a moan as she rides me with practiced sweeps of her hips. My hands cup her swollen breasts as I gaze at her in awe. I've never seen a more beautiful sight than my wife with her gently rounded belly, flushed all over and riding my cock as if her life depended on it.

It's not long before my release is bubbling to the surface, but I refuse to come without her. I know exactly what will set her off.

"Look at you riding my dick. So perfect, darlin'. Your pussy is gobbling up my cock. That greedy little thing sucking on me will have me nutting in you in no time. Better be glad you're already pregnant or this big load I got for you would sure as hell do the trick."

Her breath catches at my dirty talk. I swat her ass, and she moans, so I do it again, relishing how her ass jiggles on my cock.

"Cole!" She calls my name as her pussy flutters around my dick.

"I'm right there with you," I mutter as I hammer into her. "Fuck Emily! Here it comes, darlin'."

Emily screams as I announce my impending orgasm. My breathing becomes choked as I dump my load violently inside her.

I think I'm going to pass out from pleasure as she

rides me through our orgasms, milking more cum from me than I thought my body could produce.

When she finally collapses in my arms, shaking and spent with a thin sheen of sweat covering her body, I kiss the side of her head and stroke her blonde tresses as

I rain praises on her. My wife, my woman, and soon-to-be the mother of my child.

My everything.

THE END

Summer is the season for love at Mountain Ridge Resort! Pack your bags and get ready to have the time of your life at this charming, lakeside resort nestled in the Virginia mountains. This summer, our guests are getting much more than they expect, when what starts as a summer getaway ends in love and happily-ever-after! Your reservation is confirmed. Check in today, and join some of your favorite romance authors for 25 unforgettable, steamy, summer love stories.

Visit Emma's website to get a FREE book you can't get anywhere else: www.authoremmabray.com.